Franny K. Stein

MAD SCIENTIST

RECIPE FOR DISASTER

READ ALL OF FRANNY'S ADVENTURES

Stein

MAD SCIENTIST

RECIPE FOR DISASTER
JIM BENTON

SIMON & SCHUSTER BOOKS FOR YOUNG READERS

NEW YORK LONDON TORONTO SYDNEY NEW DELHI

SIMON & SCHUSTER BOOKS FOR YOUNG READERS

An imprint of Simon & Schuster Children's Publishing Division
1230 Avenue of the Americas, New York, New York 10020
This book is a work of fiction. Any references to historical events, real people,
or real places are used fictitiously. Other names, characters, places, and
events are products of the author's imagination, and any resemblance to
actual events or places or persons, living or dead, is entirely coincidental.
For information about special discounts for bulk purchases, please contact
Simon & Schuster Special Sales at 1-866-506-1949 or business@simonandschuster.com.
The Simon & Schuster Speakers Bureau can bring authors to your live event. For more
information or to book an event, contact the Simon & Schuster Speakers Bureau at
1-866-248-3049 or visit our website at www.simonspeakers.com.
Book design by Tom Daly
The text for this book was set in Neue Captain Kidd Lowercase.
The illustrations for this book were rendered in pen, ink, and watercolor.
Manufactured in the United States of America
0620 FFG
First Edition
2 4 6 8 10 9 7 5 3 1
Library of Congress Cataloging-in-Publication Data
Names: Benton, Jim, author.
Title: Recipe for disaster / Jim Benton.
Description: First edition. | New York : Simon & Schuster Books for Young Readers,
2020] | Series: Franny K. Stein, mad scientist ; [#9] | Audience: Ages 6-10. |
Audience: Grades 2-3. | Summary: Concerned that the fundraisers for the school
art and music departments are not doing well, Franny K. Stein creates
in her laboratory/kitchen an irresistible muffin recipe.
Identifiers: LCCN 2019048732 (print) | LCCN 2019048733 (ebook) |
ISBN 9781534413405 (hardcover) | ISBN 9781534413412 (trade paperback) |
ISBN 9781534413429 (ebook)
Subjects: CYAC: Science—Experiments—Fiction. | Muffins—Fiction. | Fund raising—
Fiction. | Schools—Fiction. | Humorous stories.
Classification: LCC PZ7.B447547 Rec 2020 (print) | LCC PZ7.B447547 (ebook) | DDC
Fic —dc23
LC record available at https://lccn.loc.gov/2019048732
LC ebook record available at https://lccn.loc.gov/2019048733

For Mary K

ACKNOWLEDGMENTS

Thanks to Kristen LeClerc, Krista Vitola,
Catherine Laudone, Tom Daly, Dorothy Gribbin,
and the rest of the S&S team,

CONTENTS

Franny K. Stein
MAD SCIENTIST

RECIPE FOR DISASTER

CHAPTER ONE

FRANNY'S HOUSE

The Stein family lived in the pretty pink house with the lovely purple shutters down at the end of Daffodil Street. Everything about the house was bright and cheery.

When you think about it, pink and purple paint look quite nice together, but that just wasn't the type of thing that Franny thought about.

In fact, Franny hardly ever thought about paint, unless you could use it to make yourself invisible, or fireproof, or if it was the kind that could make you taste terrible to monsters.

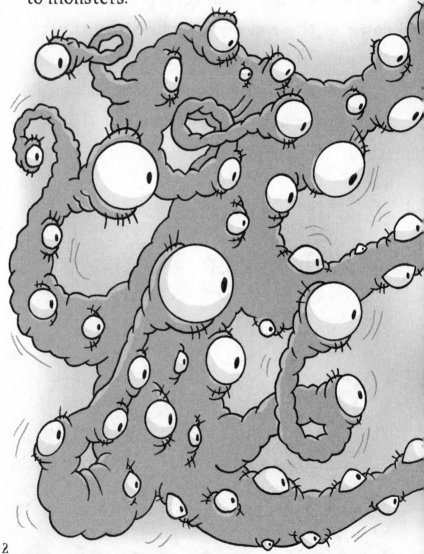

Any mad scientist will tell you that tasting too good is a *very dangerous thing.*

No, pretty much the only time she really thought about paint was when she found some on her toothbrush, which was happening more and more often since Igor had taken up a new hobby: painting.

"It's a *tooth*brush, Igor. Not a *paint*brush," she shouted from her bathroom.

Igor had been showing a real interest in art lately, and was slowly getting better at it.

He had also taken up gymnastics.

All that bouncing around was probably how the paint got on the toothbrush.

Franny didn't really mind. She wasn't very interested in art herself, but painting made Igor happy, and this hobby was a lot safer for the world than when he helped Franny with her experiments.

MUCH safer.

21

CHAPTER TWO
GET YOUR BAKED GOODS STRAIGHT

Franny watched out the window of her classroom as two workers carried a big, rusty piece of junk out of the school.

She raised her hand.

"Miss Shelly, what is that thing?"

"It looks like the old furnace," her teacher said. "I think the school is getting a nice new one. The old one never worked very well."

"They're not just going to throw that away, are they??" Franny squealed.

"I don't know what they're going to do with it, Franny—" Miss Shelly began, but before she could finish, Franny was out the door, down the hallway, and outside.

She ran toward the workers, waving her arms.

"Guys! Wait, wait! I can use that thing. Can I have it?"

They chuckled at her.

"What are you going to do with it?" one of them joked.

"I'm not sure yet," Franny said, rubbing her hands over the surface of it. "But that is some good, heavy steel. I could make a lot of stuff from this."

"Like what?" the other man asked.

"Like, I could make a small tank, I think, or maybe a rocket—maybe some kind of robot. I'll invent something."

"But this thing has already been invented," one of them said. "It's a furnace."

"Then maybe I'll reinvent it," she told them.

Miss Shelly walked out of the school to get Franny. When she got there, she found that the workers were laughing at her, and Franny didn't even seem to notice.

"This little cupcake says she wants to make a rocket out of this," one of them said to Miss Shelly with a snicker.

Miss Shelly smiled.

"She can do that, you know."

The worker sneered. He didn't believe Miss Shelly, either.

Miss Shelly's face became very serious. "You remember that giant asteroid that crashed into the earth last month and destroyed half the planet?"

"No," they said.

"That's because this little cupcake here blew it out of the sky with a rocket she made out of a broken refrigerator and an old dollhouse," Miss Shelly said proudly.

The workmen stared at Franny nervously.

"Never underestimate a little cupcake. Lots of them are real smart cookies," Miss Shelly said.

"So, can I have it?" Franny grinned.

"You may have it," Miss Shelly said, "but you have to promise not to build anything destructive."

"Nothing destructive! I promise!" Franny replied, clapping her hands. She turned to the workmen.

"Thanks SO much! Just leave it out here. I'll come back after school and get it."

"Aren't you going to need some help?" one of the workers asked. "It's pretty heavy."

"Oh, I'll have help," she said. "I have a lab assistant."

"A lab assistant?" they asked.

"Well, he's not a pure Lab," Miss Shelly added. "He's also part poodle, part Chihuahua, part beagle, part spaniel, part shepherd, and part some kind of weaselly thing that isn't even exactly a dog."

CHAPTER THREE

SALE FAIL

After school, Franny walked to the front lobby to wait for Igor to help her with the furnace.

She saw a small table with her friends Mona and Vincent behind it. They had a sign posted that said BAKE SALE.

Franny examined the things they were selling. There were some ugly oatmeal cookies, some poorly frosted cupcakes, and a pile of things that she thought were either brownies or chunks of dirt.

She picked up a plate and examined the items on it more closely.

"What are these horrible-looking things?" Franny asked. "Some kind of giant poisonous mushrooms?"

"Those are blueberry muffins," Mona said. "I made those."

"On purpose?" Franny asked.

Mona just scowled.

"Are you trying to sell these?" Franny asked.

"Yes," Mona said sadly. "We're trying to raise funds for the music and art departments. The school never has enough money for instruments or art supplies."

Franny thought for a moment.

"That's probably because that stuff isn't as important as math and science," Franny said.

They eyed her angrily.

"Let me ask you," Vincent said. "Where did you learn about gears and guts and electronics and stuff like that?"

"I learned it mostly from books," Franny said.

"Well, you know those drawings and diagrams in the books? Somebody had to draw and paint those," he said. "An artist did that."

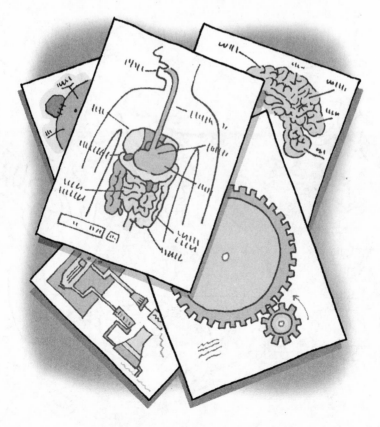

"And when you're making your robots or monsters or whatever, do you ever have music playing in the background?" Mona asked.

"I do," Franny said. "The music makes the work easier somehow. And it makes the monsters less bitey."

"Music, dance, art, entertainment — these things all make the world better. They make people happy in a way that helps everyone enjoy their jobs more," Mona said.

Franny nodded. She liked all that stuff.

"Maybe you have a point," Franny said.

Plus, Igor really liked music while he was painting or practicing gymnastics.

Franny shrugged.

"Okay, I think you're right. All of those things are important," Franny said. "Possibly *very* important."

Igor walked in and skipped up to the bake sale to look at the treats. He loved treats.

He sniffed around and then tugged on Franny's sleeve to leave.

"If Igor doesn't want something, that is not a good sign for your bake sale," Franny said. "I've seen him eat a pile of dirty socks like it was a plateful of spaghetti."

Mona's and Vincent's sad, sad faces became even sadder.

Franny couldn't just leave them like that.

"Okay, okay. Maybe I can bake some things you can sell. I'm sure I can do better than your blueberry poisonous mushroom thingies," she said.

"They're muffins," Mona said angrily.

"Igor and I need to get my furnace home, and then I'll see if I can come up with something that might help," Franny told them.

"Thanks," they said, and offered her a free cookie.

A free, gross cookie.

"I'm good," Franny said.

CHAPTER FOUR
EASY BAKE

Franny listened to some music as she stirred together cookie ingredients inside a big blue bowl.

"Seriously, Igor, how difficult can baking be? You take some flour, add some sugar, toss it in the oven, and boom! You have delicious cookies, right?"

Igor smiled and nodded. He had total faith in Franny's baking skills.

Three hours later, the kitchen was a mess, and most of the cookies Franny had made were either raw, burnt, or just plain nasty.

Only one of them had turned out okay. She dropped it in Igor's dish and let him eat it.

"I give up," Franny said. "This is too hard."

Igor ran and got a painting he had recently finished and waved it at Franny.

"You're reminding me that this is all about the art, right?" Franny said, taking off her apron.

Igor nodded.

"And how I told them I would help..."

Igor barked.

"Okay," Franny said. "I get it. We won't let our art friends down. But it's clear that I'm not much of a baker. If I'm going to do this, I'm going to have to do this MY WAY. Igor, to the laboratory!"

Igor gulped. Franny always got that look in her eye when she was about to do something *experimental.*

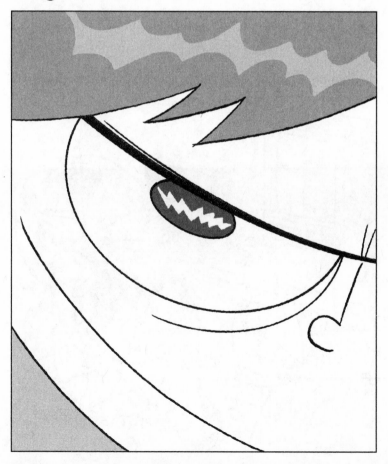

Chapter Five

THE BAKER MAKER

Franny assembled an electronic brain and downloaded every recipe on Earth into it.

She studied the fast and graceful movements of the best chefs, and constructed arms and hands that were just as confident and nimble.

She also made one of those puffy chef hats because, c'mon, those things are adorable.

Franny welded and bolted for hours, twisting and shaping the discarded furnace into a marvelous creation.

She might not have been very good at baking goodies, but if you ever needed a giant steel robot with flames shooting out of its mouth and smoke coming out of its ears, she was your girl.

And now this huge monstrosity stood before her, its inner fire burning steadily, patiently awaiting the orders of its creator.

"You're a baker," she told it.

Franny stared into its rusty metal face.

"I promised that you would never do anything destructive. You got that?"

The furnace nodded.

"Good. Now I want you to also promise that you'll make the best thing you can possibly make," she told it.

Its iron neck creaked as it nodded again.

"It should be less sweet than a cupcake, but bigger and better than a cookie," she began. "Something kids will really crave."

The machine's electronic brain hummed.

"I will make a muffin," it croaked in a hollow, mechanical voice.

"YES!" Franny cheered. "A muffin! That's perfect! Mona will love that."

The machine's inner fire crackled and grew slightly.

Franny laughed and shouted, "I shall call you . . . the Muffin Man!"

The Muffin Man's internal fire raged and he glowed with heat. As a furnace, all he ever wanted to do was to give kids exactly what they wanted. Now he knew he could do precisely that. He grinned.

"I want these muffins to be irresistible," Franny said. "They need to be perfectly delicious. We need to sell a lot of these things, Muffin Man, so do your best."

The Muffin Man nodded and got to work, carefully measuring ingredients and combining them in the proper way. They watched him, marveling at his skill with measuring cups and the way he swiftly stirred the ingredients together.

"The Muffin Man has everything under control," Franny said to Igor. "You can go paint your pictures or do gymnastics or whatever you want."

Igor wagged his tail.

"And I can get back to work on my other projects. I'm working on this one invention that lets you see into the future, and another one where you can burp into a robot's face, and it can tell you if the burp smells gross or super gross."

Igor looked at her doubtfully.

"Yeah, you're probably right. The burping one is way more fun. I'll work on that one."

And as everybody in the lab went off in different directions to do what they did best, all was just perfect in the little pink house with the lovely purple shutters, down at the end of Daffodil Street.

CHAPTER SIX

YOU CAN'T BEAT HIS BATTER

The next morning, Igor and Franny were amazed at the platters full of gorgeous muffins, beautifully wrapped in cellophane with appealing little bows.

Igor snatched one up and began unwrapping it, but Franny grabbed the muffin from him before he could take a bite.

"No, Igor. These are for the bake sale. Remember?"

She patted the Muffin Man on the back.

"Nice work," she said. "We'll take these to school and see how the kids like them. If they're popular, I may need you to make a few more."

The Muffin Man smiled. He really hoped the kids would like them. This was what he was made to do.

At the end of the day, Franny took the muffins to the table where Mona and Vincent were having another unsuccessful bake sale.

"Put these out," Franny said. "I think the kids will like them. We can give out some free samples to get them interested."

Franny crumbled a couple muffins into bite-size chunks and offered them to people passing by the table.

A first grader named Danny stopped and looked at the samples.

"Just take a taste," Franny said. "It's free."

He picked up a piece and took a tiny, cautious nibble. His eyes opened wide and he trembled. Danny clapped his hand over his mouth.

"What's wrong?" Franny said. "Is it awful?"

Danny's voice fell to a serious whisper.

"It's the most delicious thing I have ever tasted in my entire life," he said.

Then he dug deep into his pocket for the money to buy one.

The other kids saw Danny happily devouring his muffin and they were immediately curious.

After trying a sample, they also bought as many muffins as they could afford.

"This is our best sale ever!" Mona told Franny. "Thanks so much for the muffins!"

"You really are a hero," Vincent told her. "Do you think you could make some more?"

"No problem," Franny said, and smiled. "Anything to help."

Franny picked up the empty plate and headed for the door, but Danny stepped in front of her.

"Do you think there might be some muffin crumbs left on that plate?" he asked hopefully. "Could I have them?"

Franny laughed.

"Crumbs? Be serious, Danny. There will be more muffins here tomorrow."

When Franny got home, the Muffin Man was sitting quietly at the kitchen table, waiting for her.

"Well, they really loved your muffins," she told him. "I'd like you to make another batch, please."

The fire inside his internal oven became brighter and he began arranging his mixing bowls and measuring spoons.

"You better bake a dozen extra," Franny said. "If we're lucky, we might get a few more buyers tomorrow."

CHAPTER SEVEN

LUCK HAS MUFFIN TO DO WITH IT

When Franny walked into her school the next morning, there was a gigantic crowd around the bake sale table.

"What's going on?" Franny asked.

"They want the muffins," Mona said.

"They were lined up when I got here," Vincent added. "Do you have them?"

"Aren't your bake sales usually *after* school?" Franny asked them.

"Yes, but they want them NOW!" Mona shouted.

"Okay," Franny said, and she handed them the bag of muffins.

The group of kids pressed toward the table as Franny wriggled through them to get to class.

Franny walked in and took her seat.

"Your muffins certainly are popular," Miss Shelly said.

"Isn't it great?" Franny grinned. "They're raising a lot of money for the art and music classes. It won't be long before they have all the cash they need!"

That day, Franny saw kids sneaking bites of muffins during class. At lunchtime, she saw two kids eating muffins instead of the sandwiches their parents had sent with them to school.

As she was leaving for the day, Vincent and Mona stopped her in the hall.

"We could really use more of those muffins tomorrow," Mona said.

"Like, ten times as many," Vincent added.

Franny noticed some smears on their faces.

"Wait. You're not *eating* them, are you? You're supposed to be selling them, to raise money."

"We sell most of them," Mona said.

"And we always pay for the ones we eat," Vincent said. "So it's okay."

"I guess," Franny said. "As long as you pay for them."

They grinned at her.

"Okay. More muffins," she confirmed. "The Muffin Man will be delighted."

CHAPTER EIGHT

MORE BAKING. MORE DOUGH.

Franny looked at the mess the Muffin Man was making and shook her head.

"These bigger batches are taking up too much room," Franny said. "There's hardly any space for Igor to teach the monsters how to dance."

"Please!" the Muffin Man said. "Don't make me stop. My muffins make the kids happy. I never want to stop."

"I'm not going to make you stop. I just have to figure out where to put you."

"I have an idea," he said. "There's a storage room in the basement of the school. It's right next to where I used to work as a furnace. It's practically empty. We can set up my bakery there," said the Muffin Man.

"Good idea," Franny said. "After dark, we'll immediately begin moving you to the new location."

CHAPTER NINE

JUST WHAT THEY KNEADED

"You were right," Franny said to the Muffin Man. "This is a perfect place to set up your bakery. Now you can work as late as you want, and we have space to work on our other projects."

The Muffin Man slid a tray of muffins into his built-in oven.

"Just stay out of the way and be quiet," she told him. "We don't need to let everybody know that you're down here."

Igor reached for a muffin.

"No!" Franny said. "I told you before. These are for the bake sale. Keep your paws off them."

Igor nodded.

"Good night," Franny called out to the Muffin Man as they headed up the stairs, but he didn't answer back. He was concentrating on making a great big batch of muffins for all the smiling, happy kids who would be waiting for them the next morning.

Chapter Ten

IT'S BAKING
THEM CRAZY

The next morning, the bake sale table was mobbed. Almost every kid in the school was there, and they were *not* happy.

They were yelling and shouting and demanding their muffins.

Mona and Vincent collected big handfuls of money as kids bought all the muffins they could hold.

Franny was delighted.

"Wow! So many muffins! And look at all that money!"

"They are really craving these things," Mona said as she took a bite from her own muffin.

Franny looked around at the kids.

"I don't think I recognize everybody here. Are some of these kids from other schools?"

"Maybe," Vincent shouted above the crowd.

At recess, most of the kids sat on the ground, or leaned against the wall eating crumbs off their shirts.

They were too full to do anything. Only a couple of them even talked, and all they talked about was eating muffins.

Over the next few days, Franny noticed that most of the kids were eating muffins instead of their lunches, and some were complaining that their clothes didn't fit them very well anymore.

The muffin sales just kept growing, and more and more kids from other schools were showing up to buy them.

Franny caught up with Mona and Vincent after another after-school muffin sellout.

"You should have plenty of money for the art and music departments by now," Franny said.

"Probably," Mona replied. "I'm just not that interested in the money anymore."

"Yeah," Vincent added. "When I'm practicing the flute, I'm just thinking about how I could be using my mouth to eat muffins instead."

How could muffins be that important to anybody? Franny thought to herself.

On the way out of the building, Franny stopped by the art room. There were piles of unused supplies. And the music room had unopened boxes and boxes of brand-new instruments.

"This is weird," Franny said. "But I guess if they're not interested in that stuff anymore, that's up to them. And I have projects of my own waiting for me back at the lab."

After dinner and homework, Franny went to her lab and got back to work on her new inventions.

"Igor!" she shouted. "Please come here and hold these wires while I tighten this screw."

But Igor didn't come.

"IGOR!" she shouted again.

Igor didn't answer.

He wasn't painting. He wasn't practicing his gymnastics. He wasn't even playing hide-and-go-bite with the monsters.

Igor had disappeared for a few days before, so Franny didn't worry much.

Once, he'd joined the circus for a few days.

Another time he'd tried alligator wrestling.

He'd even tried to be a fashion model.

"I'm sure there's nothing to worry about," Franny said to herself. "Sometimes he just gets curious and wants to try something. He'll be back."

CHAPTER ELEVEN
MAYBE THE BAKED GOODS ARE BAKED BARS

The next day at school there was nobody at the bake sale table.

There weren't even any kids in the hallways or classrooms, either.

"Did I accidentally show up here on a Saturday again?" Franny asked herself.

"No. This is something stranger than that. I wish Igor was here to help me."

She pulled her burp-sniffing robot out of her backpack.

"I'll bet I can modify this to sniff out other things," she said, and with a few little adjustments, a couple rubber bands, and a handful of paper clips, she finished it.

"Find Igor," she told it. "Should be easy; he kind of smells like a burp." And it started sniffing its way down the hall.

The robot stopped in front of the door to the school basement and beeped.

"Down there?" she asked it, and it beeped again.

"I wonder what he's doing down there," she said, and slowly walked down the stairs.

As she headed downward, she heard the sounds of people working and she started to smell the muffins baking.

"Maybe the Muffin Man has seen Igor," she said as she came around the corner and saw exactly what was going on.

Long tables lined the basement with kids mixing ingredients and pouring them into muffin pans.

Igor was loading the pans into one of the brand-new ovens along the wall.

If this wasn't odd enough, everybody also seemed almost half asleep.

"Oh, hi, Franny," the Muffin Man said cheerfully. "Isn't this great? Do you want to help?"

"What are you doing?" she demanded.

"We're making muffins," he said. "And not just for the kids at this school. We're making them for everybody, everywhere. Soon, the whole world will get to enjoy my wonderful muffins."

Franny shook Mona's shoulder.

"Mona! Why are you doing this?"

Mona looked at her and smiled weakly.

"He pays us in muffins, Franny. If we help, we can have all the muffins we want."

"These were just supposed to be for the bake sale," Franny said. "To raise money for art supplies and musical instruments."

Mona shrugged.

"The muffins are the only thing we care about now, Franny."

"Well, I'm shutting this thing down," Franny said. "Right this minute. No more muffins."

The kids stopped what they were doing and looked at her angrily.

Even Igor growled at her.

"You don't understand, Franny," the Muffin Man said. "I used to just be the furnace here at the school."

"I know that. I built you," Franny snapped.

"I did my best to heat the school and make the kids happy. But it was always too hot for some, and too cold for others. No matter what I did, I couldn't satisfy them all."

The kids went back to working on the muffins as he spoke.

"But then you made me into a baker. And I came up with my wonderful recipe. And everybody loves it. They're all happy now."

Franny knew she couldn't just turn him off. He was too big and heavy to attack. Plus, he was burning hot. Even if she somehow managed to tip him over, his fire could burn down the school.

There were too many kids in the basement for her to start a fight with the Muffin Man. It was too dangerous. Franny had to think fast.

"Yes," Franny said, pretending to be encouraging. "You've done a great job here. I'm not surprised that people like the muffins so much. It's a spectacular recipe."

The Muffin Man smiled at her.

"Of course, the muffins would be even better if these kids had *real* skills like yours. I mean, you were *designed* to be the greatest baker — these guys are just trying to do their best."

"But I'm training them," the Muffin Man said.

"Yeah, and I'm sure they're okay. And they'll get better eventually — years from now," Franny said.

"But you taught me everything in a single night," the Muffin Man said.

"Well, yes." Franny smiled. "I'm a scientist. I use special scientific equipment. But don't worry about it. Your way is fine."

The Muffin Man thought for a moment.

"Will you help me train them to be expert bakers? You could go get your equipment. I can pay you in muffins. You can have all you want."

"I don't think so," Franny said.

"Just try one," the Muffin Man said, and he grabbed her and pushed one toward her face.

Franny struggled. She knew she did *not* want to eat one of those.

"I'm, um, full," Franny said. "I've been eating them all morning.

"But just to be nice, I'll go to my lab, grab a few things, and be right back," Franny said, pulling away from the Muffin Man's grasp. "C'mon, Igor. You can help me."

Igor looked at her and shook his head. Franny was shocked. Igor was refusing to help her! He had been eating the muffins too. He was under their spell.

"Oh. I guess you're busy," she said. "That's okay, Igor. I can do it by myself."

And Franny ran up the stairs and all the way home.

"Even Igor is hooked on those muffins!"
Franny cried.

She had been able to count on him since
the day she got him.

In some ways, she had never felt more
alone.

CHAPTER TWELVE

SMART COOKIES DON'T CRUMBLE

Franny dug through a box of inventions. "I have **NO IDEA** what to do! I mean, my Octagonner will turn the Muffin Man into an octopus, but what if that lets him bake things four times as fast?" she wondered.

"I could just launch him to the moon in a rocket, but the kids all know the recipe now, and they'll just keep making muffins on their own — and I'm *not* sending all those kids to the moon with him.

"I suppose I could just lock them all down there in the basement, and at least they couldn't give muffins to anybody else. But that wouldn't be fair. It's not really their fault.

"I've always known how to fight great
big monsters, but this is different."

Franny sat down and looked at a painting
that Igor had done of himself and smiled.

"I guess he'll never paint one of me now,"
she said sadly.

"Wait a second," she said. "Even if I can't convince them to get rid of those muffins, I might know who can!"

And in a flash, Franny was running back to the school basement.

CHAPTER THIRTEEN

HAVE YOU SEEN, MUFFIN MAN?

In the short time Franny had been gone, the muffins were already piling up in the lobby and spilling out the doors of the school. It wouldn't be long before the Muffin Man really did have enough for the whole world.

She made her way back down into the basement.

"Looks like you are really cooking," she said with a nervous laugh.

Igor whirled round and eyed her suspiciously. Muffins were all that mattered to him now, and he knew that Franny could be very tricky.

"I, um, brought a special helmet," Franny said, pulling the invention out of her backpack. "It will let us download all of your awesome baking skills into the brains of all your helpers here."

"That sounds wonderful," the Muffin Man said. "Who should go first?"

"Oh, anybody, I guess," Franny said. "How about Mona?"

Igor let out a low growl.

Franny positioned the helmet on top of Mona's head and smiled at the Muffin Man.

"Pretty soon she'll be almost as good at baking as you," she said.

Mona smiled at Franny and said, "That's perfect. I always wanted to be a muffin maker."

"I thought you always wanted to be an artist?" Franny whispered to her, and she shrugged.

Igor began to move toward them.

Franny leaned in close so that nobody but Mona could hear her.

"Mona, this is my Visualizer Helmet. When I turn this on, you're going to get a look at the future that awaits you. You're going to see what these muffins will bring you."

"I'll bet it's going to be great," Mona said.

"Now visualize your future, Mona," Franny said, and she flipped the switch.

Mona saw herself as a teenager, making muffins and selling them to people. She did not look very happy.

As the helmet hummed, she saw farther into her future. She looked even worse — she was alone and her brushes and canvases were unused in the corner. She looked sick.

She saw her little brother and her friends eating the muffins, and never accomplishing much more than that.

She got older and older and it never got better.

A tear rolled down her cheek.

"You're right. I *did* want to be an artist," she whimpered.

Franny took the helmet off her.

"Franny, I don't want to do this anymore. I don't want to do this to myself."

"Just keep these thoughts to yourself for now," Franny told her softly, "and go get Vincent."

Soon Vincent was visualizing his future. He wasn't a musician. He wasn't really anything. He was just an unhappy adult who had sold his flute to buy muffins.

Franny took off the helmet and told him to do just as Mona had done, and to bring another kid over.

But then Franny heard Igor behind her, snarling.

"You know that I'm up to something, don't you?" she said, reaching for a muffin.

"You're right, Igor. I am. I've figured out how to make these muffins *even better*," she said, and she dropped one into the helmet.

He was still suspicious, but he knew that Franny was smart enough to make anything better.

"Just try it," she said, and she held out the helmet like it was his old, familiar dog dish.

Igor sniffed cautiously and then slowly stuck his face into the helmet.

Suddenly, Franny pulled it over his head and turned it on.

Igor saw his future.

He was an old dog now, missing some teeth and living on the streets.

He limped along, whining and groaning. He had no home, no muffins, and worst of all, no Franny.

No Franny.

He pulled his head out of the helmet. He couldn't look at her. He was ashamed of himself.

Franny hugged him.

"It's okay," she said. "You understand now."

Igor nodded.

Franny snuck around, carefully putting the helmet on each kid, revealing to them what their future would hold if they kept eating the muffins—their hopes of being doctors, lawyers, athletes, dancers . . . the muffins destroyed all of those dreams.

Each kid tore off their apron and threw down their spoon and mixing bowl.

"WE QUIT!!" they shouted.

CHAPTER FOURTEEN

KISS THE COOK (GOOD-BYE)

The fire inside the Muffin Man blazed and his eyes glowed with menacing orange flames.

"It's over, Muffin Man," Franny said, and she gestured toward the kids who were shoveling the muffins into the trash.

"They realize now what you're making them sacrifice. Your muffins are history."

The Muffin Man laughed a hollow, metallic laugh.

"You think this is the end?" he roared. "This muffin recipe is *perfect*. I'm going to share this with the whole world. Even if these kids have stopped eating them for now, they'll start again. And then I'll make EVERYBODY EVERYWHERE HAPPY."

Franny looked at Igor.

"You remember any of your gymnastics?" she asked him, and she hoisted him onto her shoulders.

With a jump and a twist, Igor flipped through the air and shoved the humming Visualizer Helmet down on the head of the Muffin Man.

The Muffin Man stood in a state of shock as the Visualizer Helmet showed him a vision of his future.

It was a sad, bleak future where people shuffled around aimlessly. They ate nothing but his muffins, and they did it without joy.

It was a horrible, unhappy world that he had created, and the Muffin Man couldn't bear to look at it.

He slowly removed the helmet.

"But . . . I promised never to do anything destructive," he said sorrowfully.

He dropped the helmet to the ground.

"I promised to make the best thing I possibly could."

The Muffin Man slouched and the fire inside him shrank to just a few glowing embers.

"My muffins don't really make people happy, do they?" he asked Franny.

"At first, they *think* they're happy," she said. "But that doesn't last long. People are usually happiest when they're creating things, or learning things, or trying to make the world or themselves better."

The Muffin Man nodded.

"No more muffin making," he said. And he dropped his little chef's hat and shuffled away, clinking and clanking up the stairs.

"He's gone!" Mona said. "You beat him, Franny!"

The kids cheered.

"It wasn't me," Franny said. "I knew I could *never* beat him. You all wanted those muffins so badly, it was clear that I could never make you stop."

She lifted the Visualizer Helmet.

"But I wondered if maybe you could make yourselves stop, once you took a look at your futures. I think that's what stopped him, too.

"He was programmed to try to make the best thing he possibly could, and to never be destructive. Once he understood what he had done, he made himself stop.

"I think that sometimes we're our own biggest heroes," Franny said as she and Igor walked up the stairs and headed home.

When they got back to the lab, Franny put her stuff away.

"I wonder where the Muffin Man went," Franny said.

Igor shrugged and hugged Franny hard. He felt bad about growling at her and she knew it.

"It's okay," she said.

CHAPTER FIFTEEN

HE IS JUST KILN IT

Franny walked happily into school the next morning. She was looking forward to a perfectly normal day with her friends.

But she didn't see any of them anywhere.

Not in the halls, not in the classrooms.

"Oh NO!" she shouted. "Did they get back to those muffins?"

She ran downstairs to the basement.

All of the muffins were gone and every-thing had been cleaned up.

"Where is everybody?" she said to her-self, and started wandering the halls.

Soon she heard laughter coming from the art room.

The kids were crowded around the Muffin Man and clapping.

"Get away from him!" Franny shouted. "He's dangerous!" She pulled the Octagonner from her backpack. She had brought it just in case something like this happened. You never know when you might have to turn somebody into an octopus.

She started pushing her way through the crowd.

"He's not dangerous," Mona said. "He's a kiln now. You know, so we can bake things out of clay."

"I reinvented myself," the Muffin Man said. "I heard somebody say I could be reinvented, so I thought for a long time and I realized I could make more people happy by doing this."

"Now we can make all sorts of things," Vincent said. "He fires them inside his belly."

"Look, I made something already!" the Muffin Man said.

He blew hard on it to cool it off and handed it to Franny.

It was a little ceramic plate with a picture of a muffin on it and the words: THANKS, FRANNY.

"It's a muffin plate!" he said.

Franny looked at it uncomfortably.

"Not for MY muffins," he laughed. "I don't do that anymore. It's for one of those nasty, ugly ones that Mona makes."

Franny laughed and threw her arm around Mona.

"Now that I think about it, Mona, I really like your muffins the best of all!"